WHALES

WHALES

MAURA GOUCK

THE CHILD'S WORLD

DESIGN
Bill Foster of Albarella & Associates, Inc.

PHOTO CREDITS
James Watt/EarthViews: back cover, 9
Howard Hall: 2
Richard Sears/EarthViews: 6, 15
Marty Snyderman: 11, 28
Marc Webber/Earthviews: 12
Flip Nicklin/Nicklin and Associates: front cover, 16, 19, 21, 23, 24
Stephen Leatherwood/EarthViews: 27
Pieter Folkens/EarthViews: 31

Printed in the United States of America.

Distributed to schools and libraries
in the United States by
ENCYCLOPAEDIA BRITANNICA EDUCATIONAL CORP
310 South Michigan Ave.
Chicago, Illinois 60604

Library of Congress Cataloging-in-Publication Data
Gouck, Maura.
Whales/Maura Gouck.,
p. cm. — (Child's World Wildlife Library)
Summary: Describes the physical characteristics and behavior of
whales and discusses several species.
ISBN 0-89565-717-1
1. Whales — Juvenile literature. [1. Whales.] I. Title.
II. Series. 91-12508
QL737.C4G58 1991 CIP
599.5—dc20 AC

For Ozzie and David

This tail belongs to the largest animal that has ever lived on earth. It is the tail of a blue whale. The other end of this whale is very deep in the water. Blue whales are enormous. Some blue whales are 100 feet long and weigh more than 150 tons. That's heavier than a dozen elephants. Of course, not all whales are giants, but even the smallest whales are larger than people.

You don't want to be too near the humpback whale while it's breaching. When it breaches, the male humpback hurls its huge body out of the water, like a rocket lifting off. Then the whale turns in the air and falls backward as its long flippers reach out. The whale lands with a tremendous splash that can be heard miles away. No one really knows why whales breach. Maybe the male whale is trying to attract a female whale . . . or maybe this is how he catches his food . . . or maybe it just feels good.

Are you wondering how a huge whale can lift its body completely out of the water? Well, having a large, strong tail helps. You can see that the tail of this whale has two halves. These are called *flukes*. The flukes lie sideways across the whale's body, like the tail of an airplane. Because it is shaped this way, the whale moves its tail up and down, not back and forth like a fish. When the whale's muscles pull the flukes up, the tail pushes the whale through the water.

Even though they live in water, whales breathe air just like people. A whale breathes through a hole in the top of its head. This is called a *blowhole*. Some whales have a single blowhole. Others have a split hole that looks like our nostrils.

When a whale comes to the surface, it opens the blowhole and lets out the old air. The air has been inside the whale, so it is warm and moist. When it comes out, it looks like a waterspout. After the whale breathes fresh air, it closes the blowhole and dives back under the water. Some whales can stay below the surface for more than an hour before coming up for another breath.

This is a mother whale and her baby, which is called a *calf*. A whale calf stays close to its mother for the first year of life. Luckily, mother whales don't have to carry their young because, even at birth, most baby whales weigh more than 1,000 pounds.

It may not look it, but a whale calf is like a human baby in some ways. It develops inside the mother and is born alive. It also drinks its mother's milk just like a human baby. Of course, a baby whale drinks a lot more than a human baby. Some baby whales drink over 100 gallons of milk a day. That's more than a human baby drinks in a year!

This strange-looking whale is a narwhal. It is a small whale with a body about the length of a car. A lot of people think that's a horn attached to its nose, but it's not. It's actually a tooth that grows through a hole in the narwhal's lip. As the tooth grows, it twists around and around and ends up looking like a screw. A narwhal's tooth can grow up to 10 feet long. No one knows why the narwhal has this tooth. It may be for fighting or for communicating with other narwhals. One thing this tooth probably is not used for is chewing.

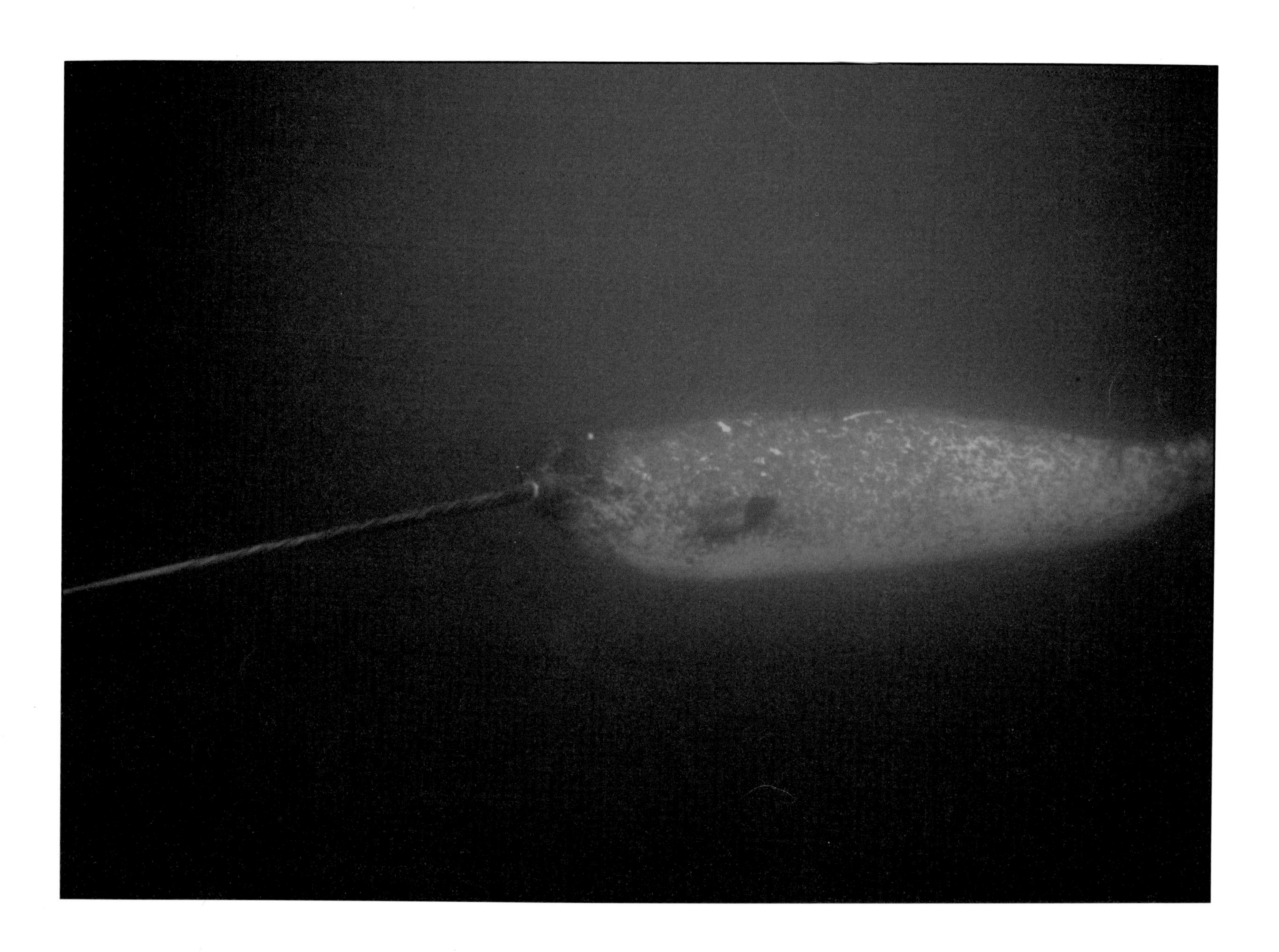

Another peculiar-looking whale is the very large sperm whale. This whale has a square-shaped head that seems much too big for the narrow mouth underneath it. The sperm whale is a mystery to scientists. Inside its head is a huge lump of material that contains enough oil to fill many barrels. For many years sperm whales were killed for their oil. Before there were electric lamps, people used the oil to make candles. Today, there's no need for this, and laws protect these whales from hunters.

The animal named "killer whale" sounds like a huge creature that you should avoid. Even though some killer whales grow to 20 feet long, this is small compared with a sperm or blue whale. If you prefer, you can call this black-and-white whale "orca," which is its other name.

Killer whales are popular performers at marine parks. They are trained to do tricks and even let their trainers ride on their backs. So how do you suppose a friendly animal like this got a name like "killer"? It's probably because of what it eats. Like other whales, the killer whale eats lots of fish, but it also eats other animals like seals and penguins. Don't worry. Killer whales have never shown any interest in attacking humans.

Like many other whales, killer whales travel in groups called *pods*. A pod is like a large family of adult and young whales. Even when a baby killer whale grows up, it seems to stay with the same pod.

From this bird's-eye view, you can see about 10 killer whales, but killer whale pods sometimes have as many as 50 members. Other types of whales also travel in pods, and some of these pods have thousands of whales. That's more like a whole town than a family.

This diver is swimming alongside a right whale. The whale got its name because hunters said it was the "right" whale to hunt. It moved slowly and was easier to catch than other kinds of whales. The hunters would wait for the whale to come up to breathe. When they saw the water spouting from the blowhole, the whalers would yell, "Thar she blows," and the chase would begin. So many right whales were killed for their blubber, whalebone, and meat that people were afraid they would all disappear. Laws were made to stop people from hunting them.

Today boats following whales are filled with people who are hoping to see a whale up close and maybe even touch one. Because whales are gentle and let people get near them, we have been able to study them and learn many things about how they live. There is still a lot more we want to know about whales. How intelligent are they? How do they communicate? How do they learn? Some people are asking an even more important question about whales. How can we protect these animals so they don't disappear from the waters of the earth?